Carla's Talent Show

written by Kimberly Beckley
illustrated by Valorie Totire

Carla's teacher, Mrs. Anderson, announced, "In two weeks we are going to have a school talent show."

Carla was so excited. She couldn't wait to tell her mom.

On the way home from school, Carla saw a dance studio. She went inside and sat down to watch the dancers.

The ballet dancers danced across the floor.
"They're too quiet," thought Carla.

The jazz dancers danced across the floor.
"They're too fast," thought Carla.

The tap dancers danced across the floor. They were wearing tall, black hats and long coattails.

Carla listened to the tap, tap of their dance shoes. "I'm going to tap-dance for the school talent show," she thought.

Carla ran the rest of the way home to tell her mom about the talent show.

"Mom, Mom, I'm going to tap-dance for the school talent show!" said Carla.

"First, you need to call Aunt Gigi and ask her if she will teach you how to tap-dance. Then we will have to go to the store and buy you a pair of tap shoes," said Mom.

"Okay, Mom," said Carla.

Carla smiled and hung up the phone.

"Aunt Gigi said I can go to her house every day after school and she will teach me how to tap-dance," said Carla.

Carla and her mom went to the store to buy a pair of tap shoes. Carla picked out a pair of black patent leather tap shoes.

The salesperson laced red ribbons through the tap shoes and tied two big bows.

Carla made a tap, tap with her tap shoes. "These are the perfect tap shoes," she smiled.

Every day after school, Carla went to Aunt Gigi's house to learn to tap-dance.

Carla practiced her act until it was perfect.

NEW YORK

Mom and Aunt Gigi went to see Carla tap-dance in the talent show. They took their cameras and sat in the front row.

Mrs. Anderson announced, “Next is Carla. She will be tap-dancing.”

Talent
Show

Carla walked on stage wearing her tall, black hat; long coattails; and black patent leather tap shoes laced with red bows.

The stage lights shined brightly on Carla.

Carla winked at Aunt Gigi and began to tap-dance just as Aunt Gigi had taught her. Carla smiled and she danced perfectly.

Carla was the star of the talent show.